For Erica, who always knew I could fly

THIS IS A BORZOI BOOK PUBLISHED BY ALFRED A. KNOPF

Copyright © 2015 by Karl Newsom Edwards

Visit us on the Web! randomhousekids.com

Educators and librarians, for a variety of teaching tools, visit us at RHTeachersLibrarians.com

Library of Congress Cataloging-in-Publication Data

Edwards, Karl, author, illustrator.

Fly! / written and illustrated by Karl Newsom Edwards. — First edition.

p.   cm.

Summary: "A young fly imitates his garden insect friends to try to figure out what he's best at."
—Provided by publisher

ISBN 978-0-385-39283-9 (trade) — ISBN 978-0-385-39284-6 (lib. bdg.) —
ISBN 978-0-553-49654-3 (ebook)

[1. Flies—Fiction. 2. Insects—Fiction. 3. Ability—Fiction.] I. Title.

PZ7.E25635FI 2015 [E]—dc23 2014002391

The text of this book is set in many fonts, but Fly speaks in Abadi 35 point and Spoleto.

The illustrations were created digitally.

MANUFACTURED IN CHINA

March 2015

10 9 8 7 6 5 4 3 2 1

First Edition

KARL NEWSOM EDWARDS

Fly!

Alfred A. Knopf
New York

WIGGLE!

wiggle?

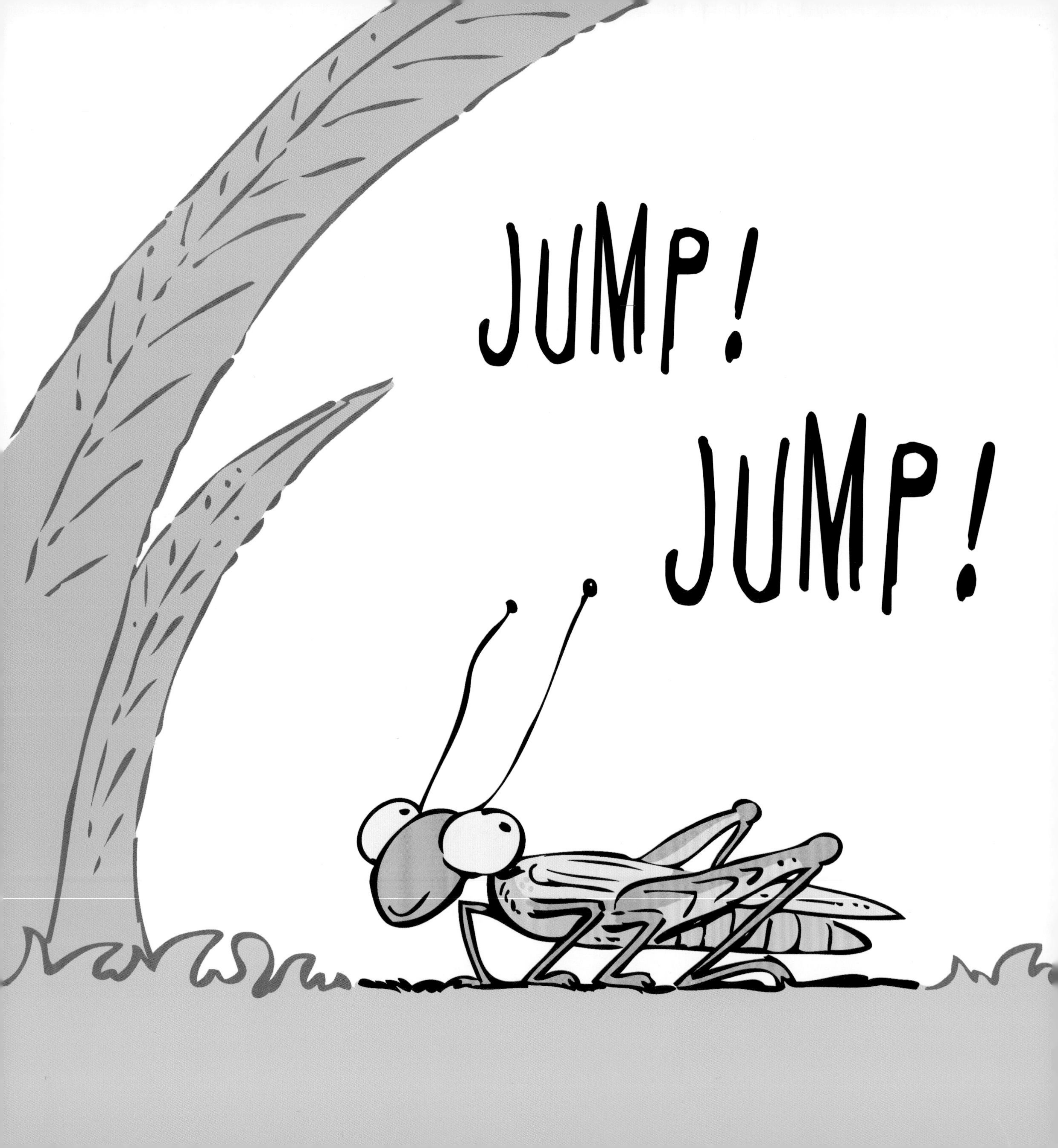
JUMP!
JUMP!

jump?

ROLL!

MARCH! MARCH! MARCH!

swing?

CHOMP!
CHEW!

chomp? chew?

Dig!

dig?

Buzz!

FLUTTER!

FLUTTER!

FLIT!
FLIT!

buzz? flutter? flit?

fly?

Yes! Fly!

Bug Facts

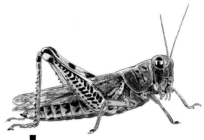

jump!

Grasshoppers can jump up to 20 times their own length. If you were a grasshopper, you could jump over a two-story house.

fly!

Flies have sticky pads on their feet that help them walk upside down!

roll!

Pill bugs, also known as roly-polies, curl into tight balls when they're scared.

wiggle!

Worms don't like the light because it dries them out. If they feel heat, they wiggle away!

march!

Ants can lift up to 20 times their own body weight. If you were as strong as an ant, you would be able to pick up a cow!

swing!

Some spiders weave together strands of silk that act as parachutes, capable of taking them high above the world. This is called ballooning.

chomp! chew!

Caterpillars are always hungry and can eat for two days straight without rest!

buzz!

Bees do a special dance called the waggle dance to let their friends know where the sweet nectar is!

flutter!

Butterflies have four wings, but they can't fly if they're cold.

dig!

When beetles rub their wing covers against their body, it makes a hissing squeak.

flit!

Dragonflies can fly straight up and down and forward and backward, and hover like a helicopter.